5.88

DATE DUE

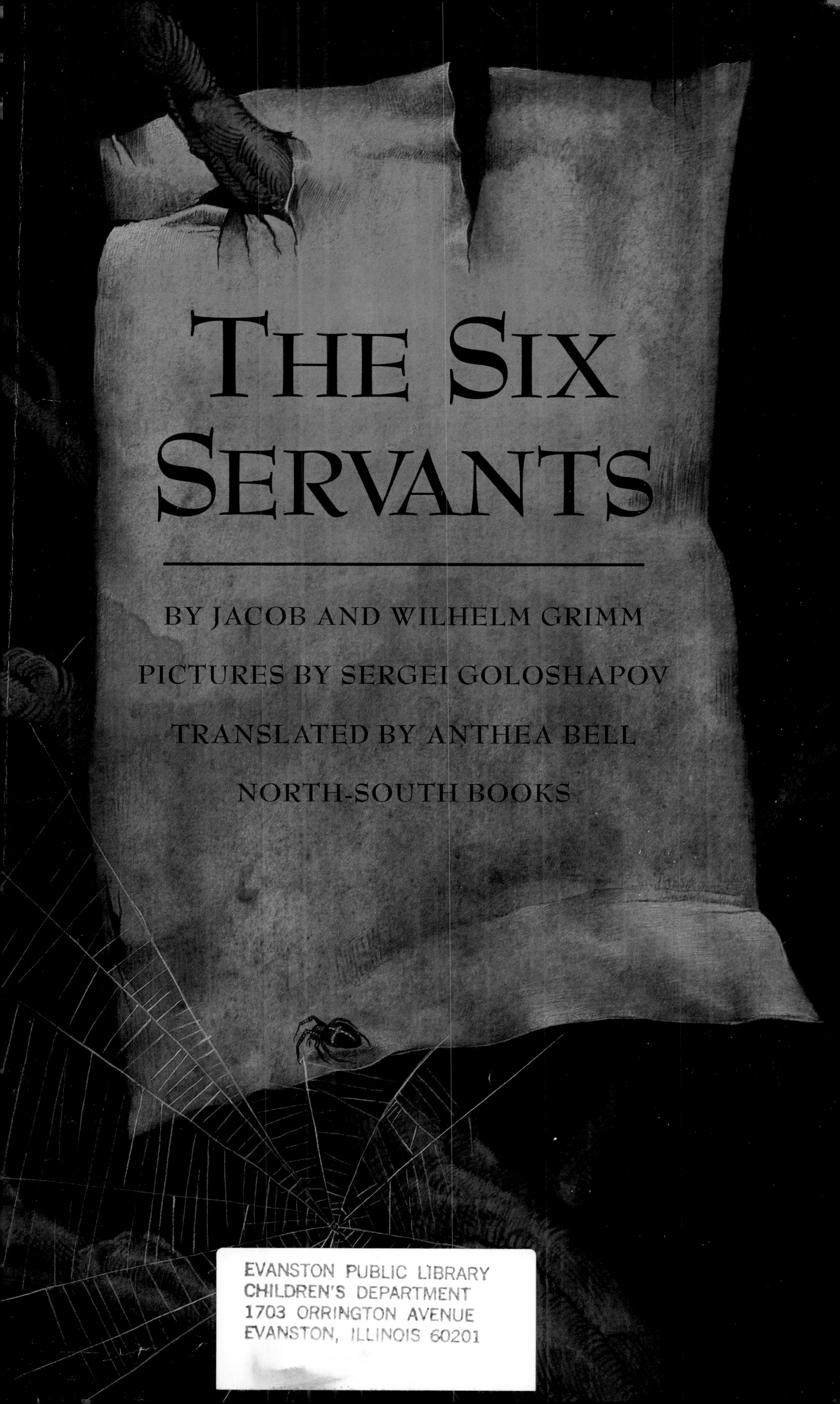

The Six Servants

By Jacob and Wilhelm Grimm

Pictures by Sergei Goloshapov

Translated by Anthea Bell

North-South Books

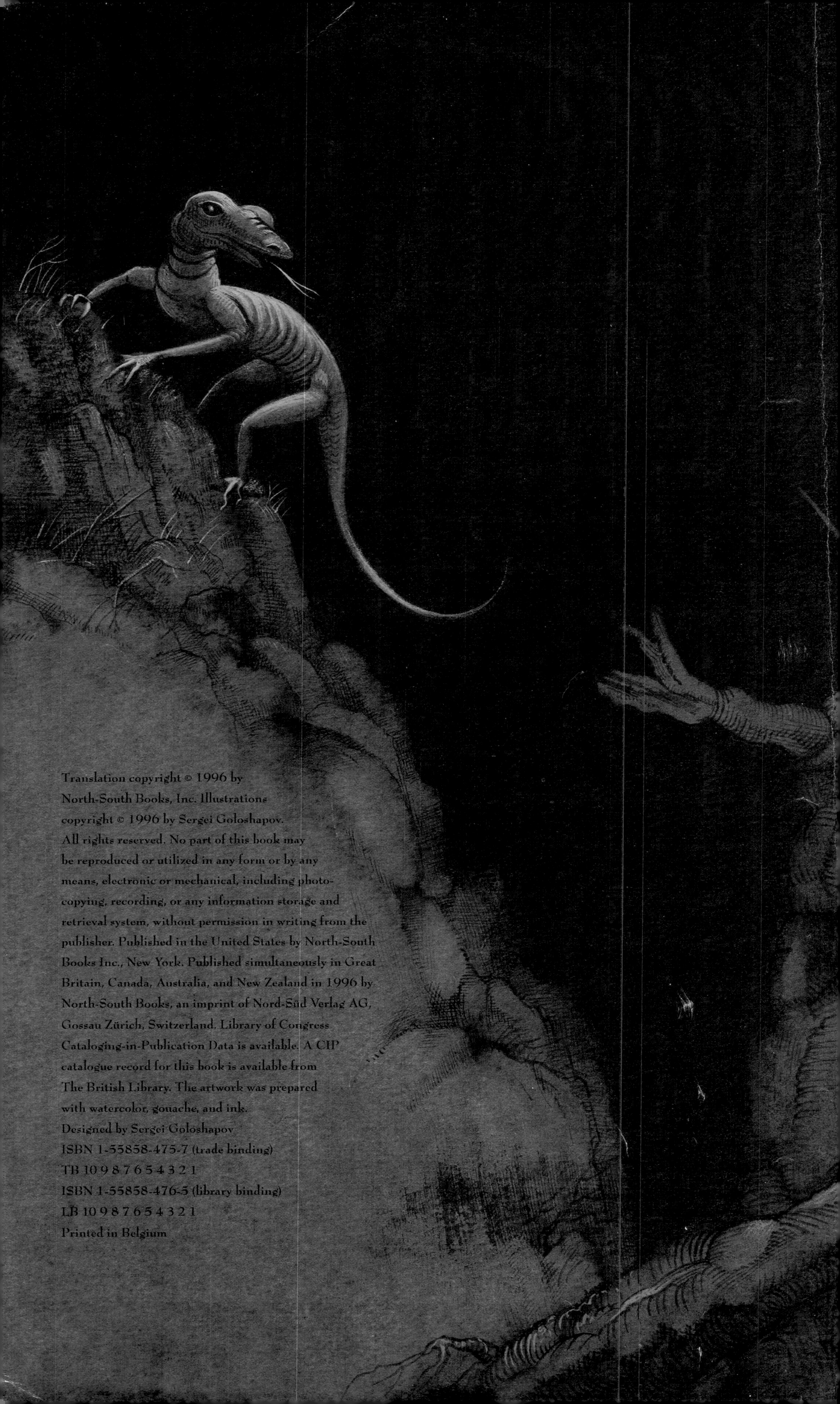

 Published in the United States by North-South Books Inc., New York. Published simultaneously in Great Britain, Canada, Australia, and New Zealand in 1996 by North-South Books, an imprint of Nord-Süd Verlag AG, Gossau Zürich, Switzerland. Library of Congress Cataloging-in-Publication Data is available. A CIP catalogue record for this book is available from The British Library. The artwork was prepared with watercolor, gouache, and ink.
Designed by Sergei Goloshapov
ISBN 1-55858-475-7 (trade binding)
TB 10 9 8 7 6 5 4 3 2 1
ISBN 1-55858-476-5 (library binding)
LB 10 9 8 7 6 5 4 3 2 1
Printed in Belgium

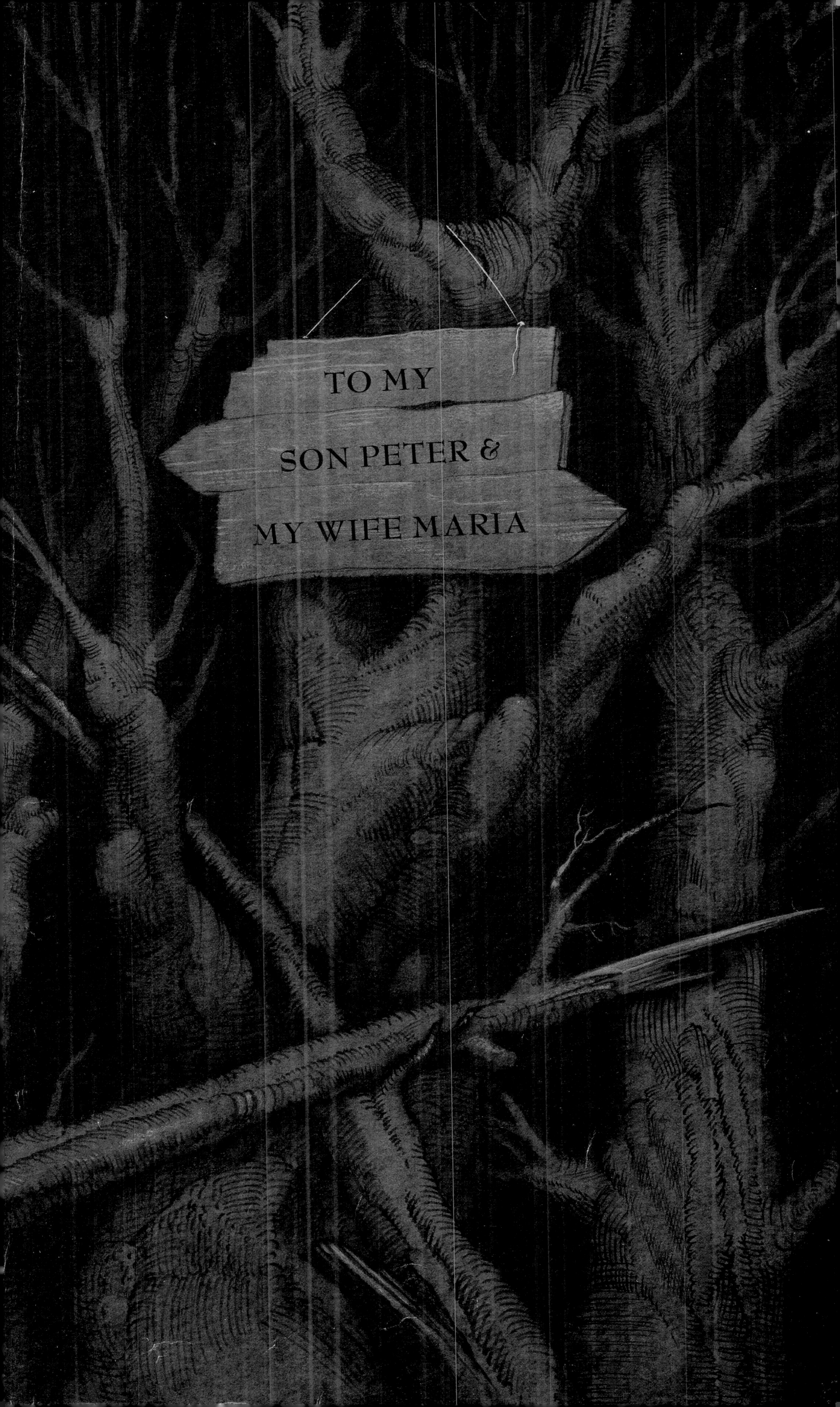
TO MY
SON PETER &
MY WIFE MARIA

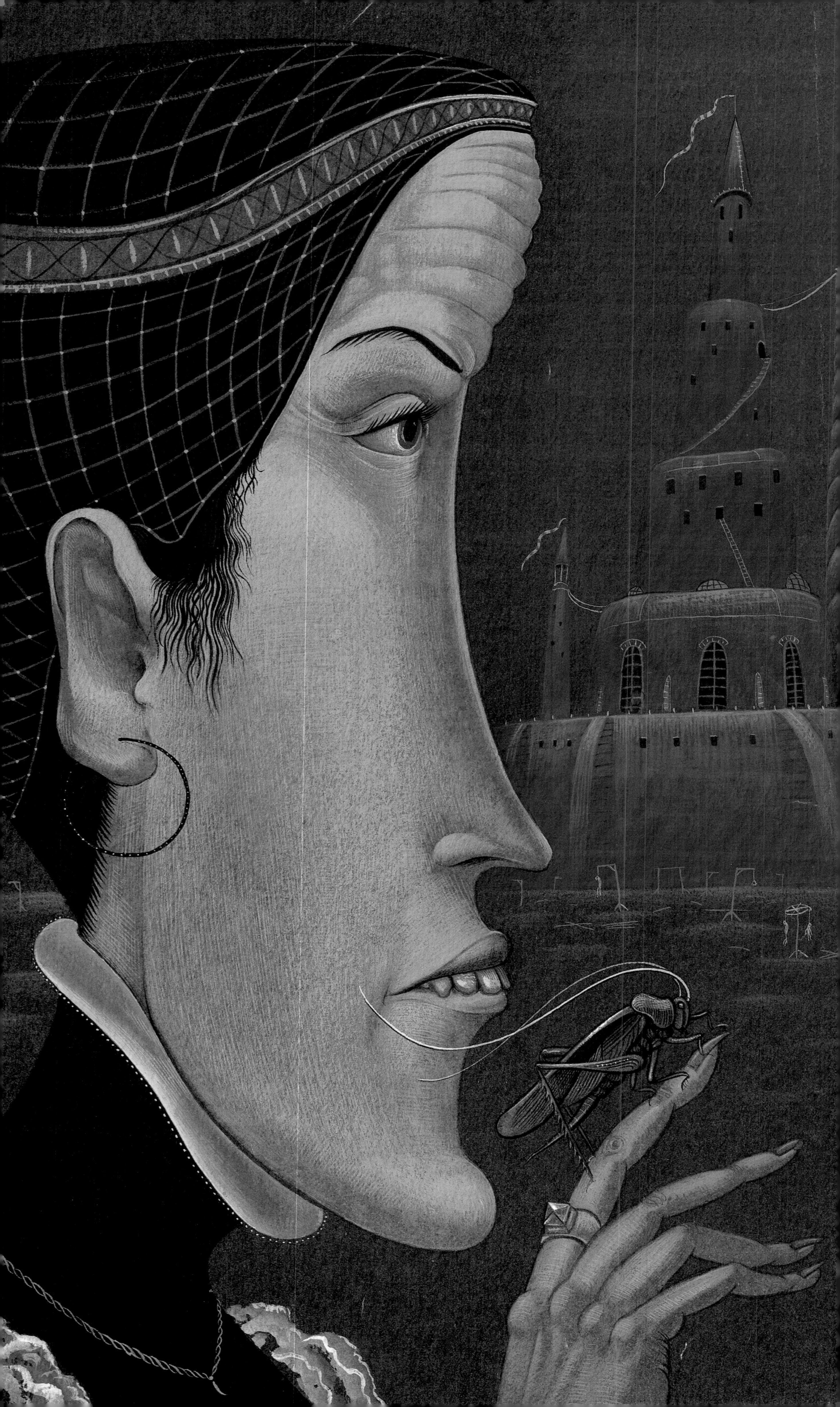

ONCE UPON A TIME

there was an old queen who was an enchantress, and her daughter was the loveliest girl under the sun. The old woman thought of nothing but how to lure men to their doom, and when anyone came courting her daughter, she said that if he wanted to marry the princess, she would set him a task, and he must perform it or die. Dazzled by the girl's beauty, many men tried their luck, but they could not perform the task the old woman set them, so their heads were cut off.

Now there was a king's son who heard of the girl's great beauty, and he said to his father, "Let me go and try to win her hand."

"Never!" said the king. "If you go, you'll be going to your death."

At that the prince took to his bed and lay there for seven years, mortally sick. Not a doctor in the land could cure him. When his father saw there was no hope left, he said sadly, "Go and try your luck, then. I can't think of any other way to help you."

So the prince got up, perfectly well again, and set off cheerfully on his way.

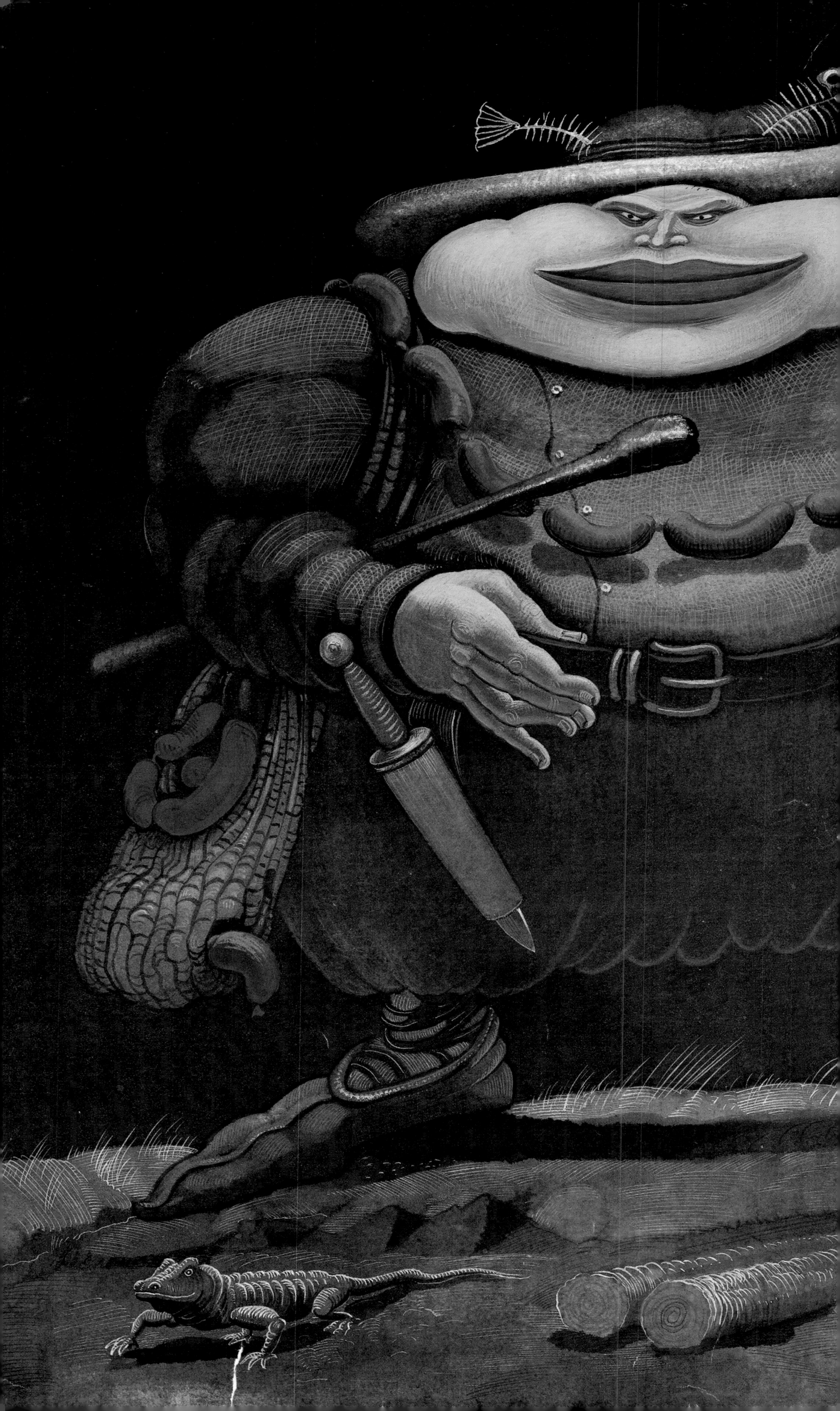

As he was riding over the moors, he saw something in the distance like a large haystack on the ground. Coming closer, he found that it was really the stomach of a man lying flat on his back, but a stomach as large as a little mountain. At the sight of the prince, the fat man stood up and said, "If you need a servant, hire me."

"What would I do with a great hulk like you?" said the prince.

"Oh, this is nothing!" said the fat man. "Why, if I really puff myself out, I'm three thousand times as fat as this!"

"If that's so," said the prince, "I believe I could use your services, so come along with me."

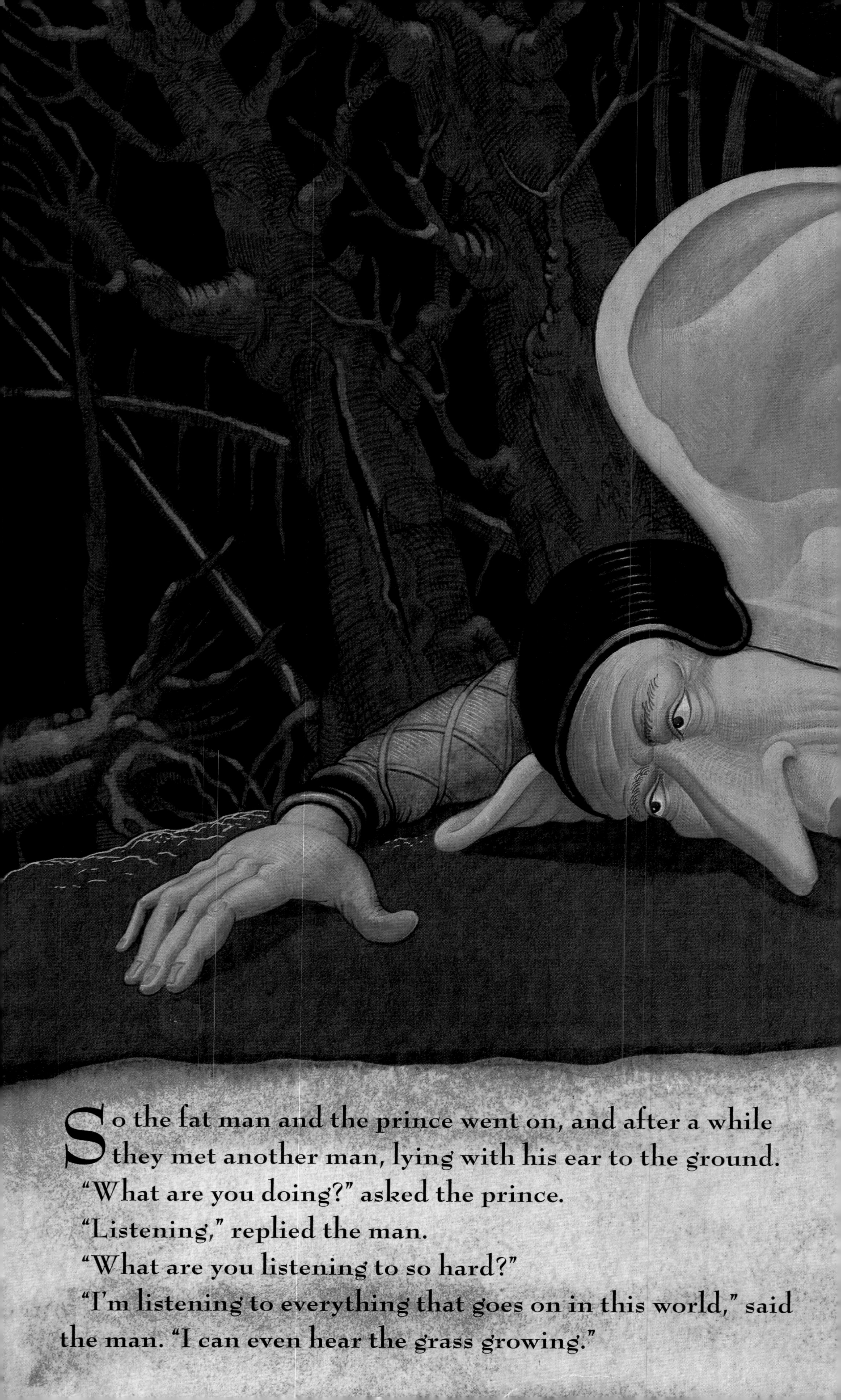

So the fat man and the prince went on, and after a while they met another man, lying with his ear to the ground.

"What are you doing?" asked the prince.

"Listening," replied the man.

"What are you listening to so hard?"

"I'm listening to everything that goes on in this world," said the man. "I can even hear the grass growing."

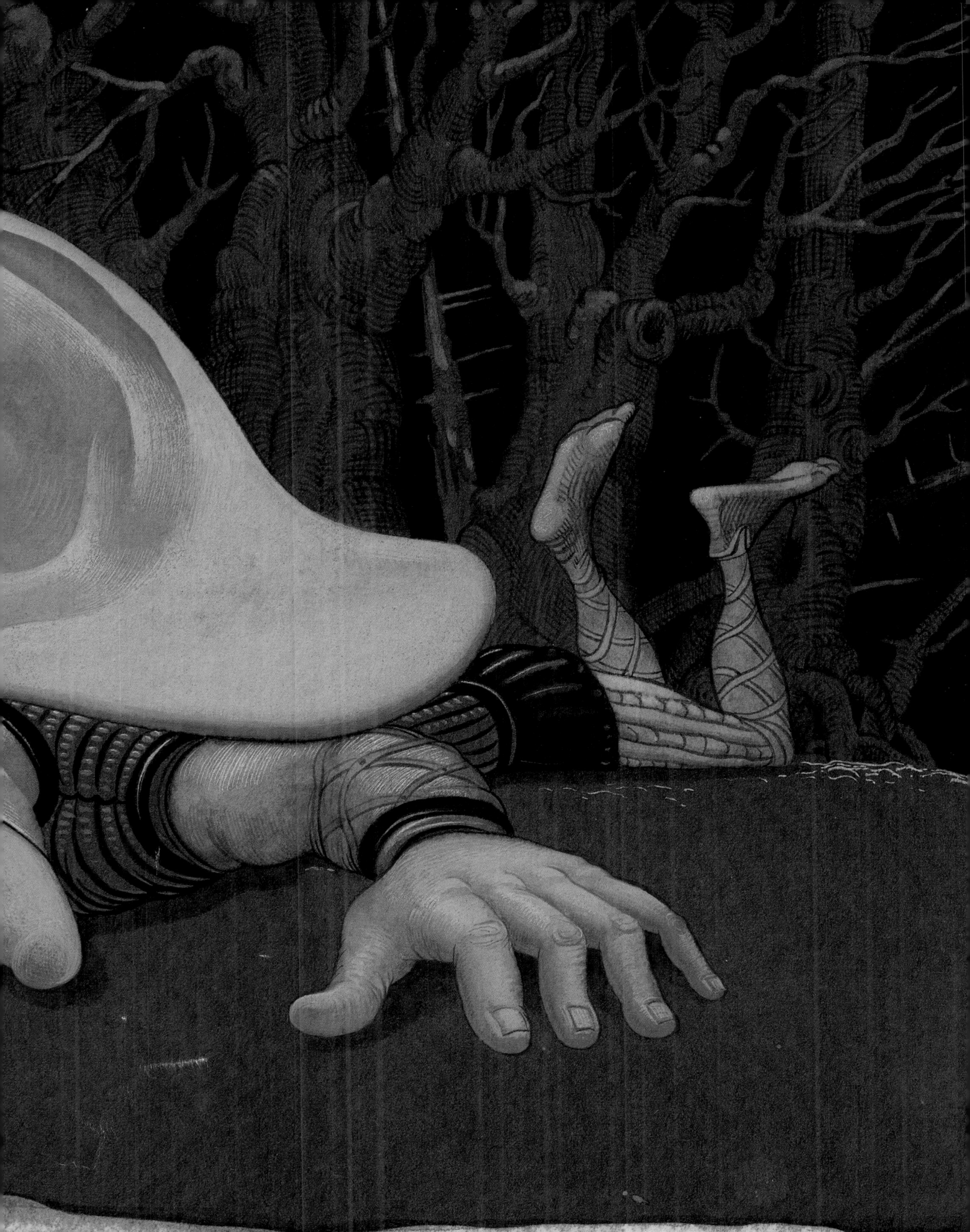

"Tell me," said the prince, "what do you hear at the court of the old queen with the beautiful daughter?"

"I hear a sword whistling through the air to cut off the head of one of the girl's suitors," said the man.

"I believe I could use your services," said the prince, "so come along with me."

Then they went on, and
they came to a pair of feet
lying on the ground, and part of
the legs belonging to them, but they
couldn't see to the end of those legs.
When they had gone some way, they
reached the man's body, and finally
they came to his head.

"Why, what a long, tall fellow you are!"
said the prince.

"Oh, this is nothing," said the long, tall
man. "If I really stretch, I'm three thousand
times as long, and taller than the highest
mountain on earth. I'd gladly serve you if you
will hire me."

"Yes, I can use your services," said the prince,
"so come along with me."

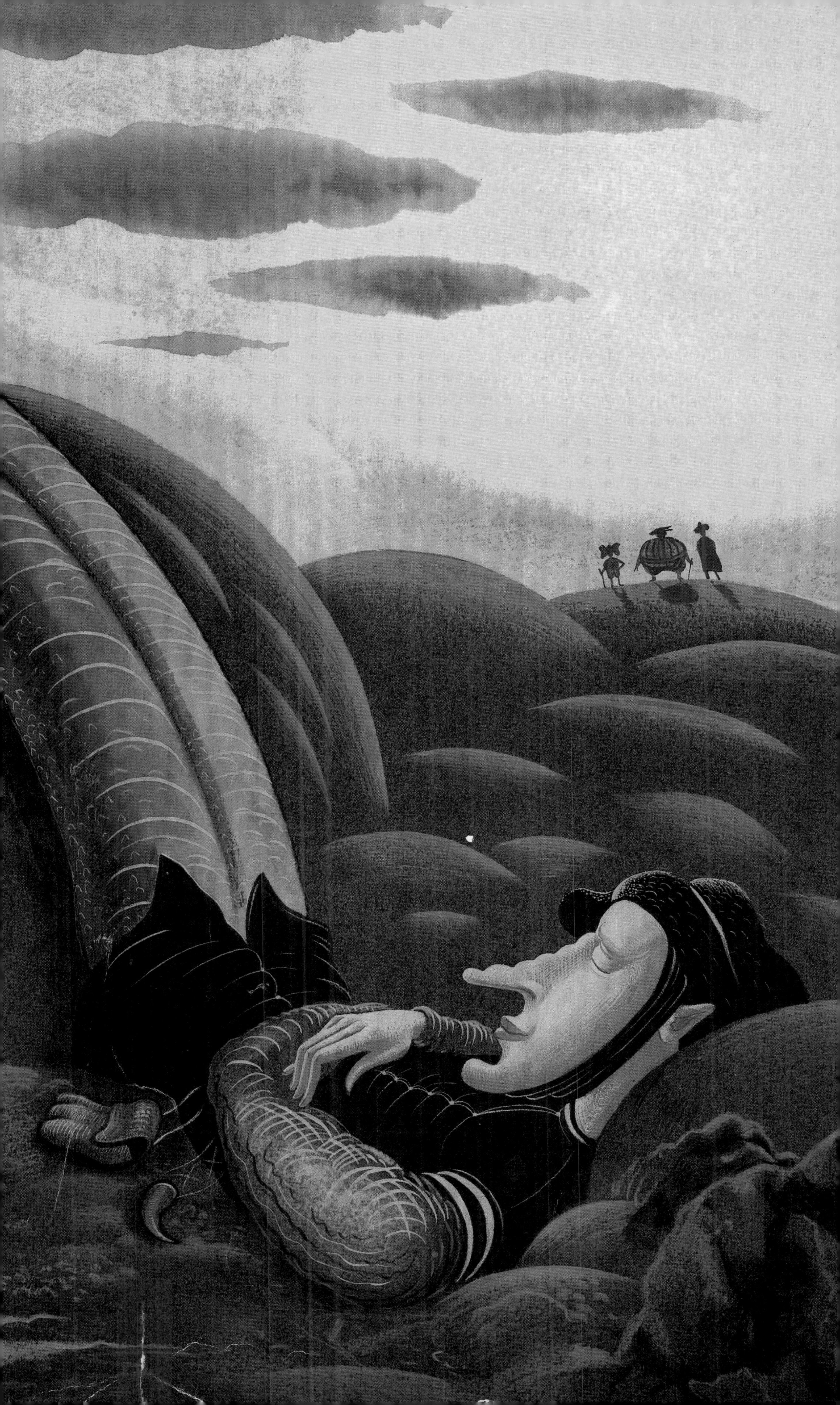

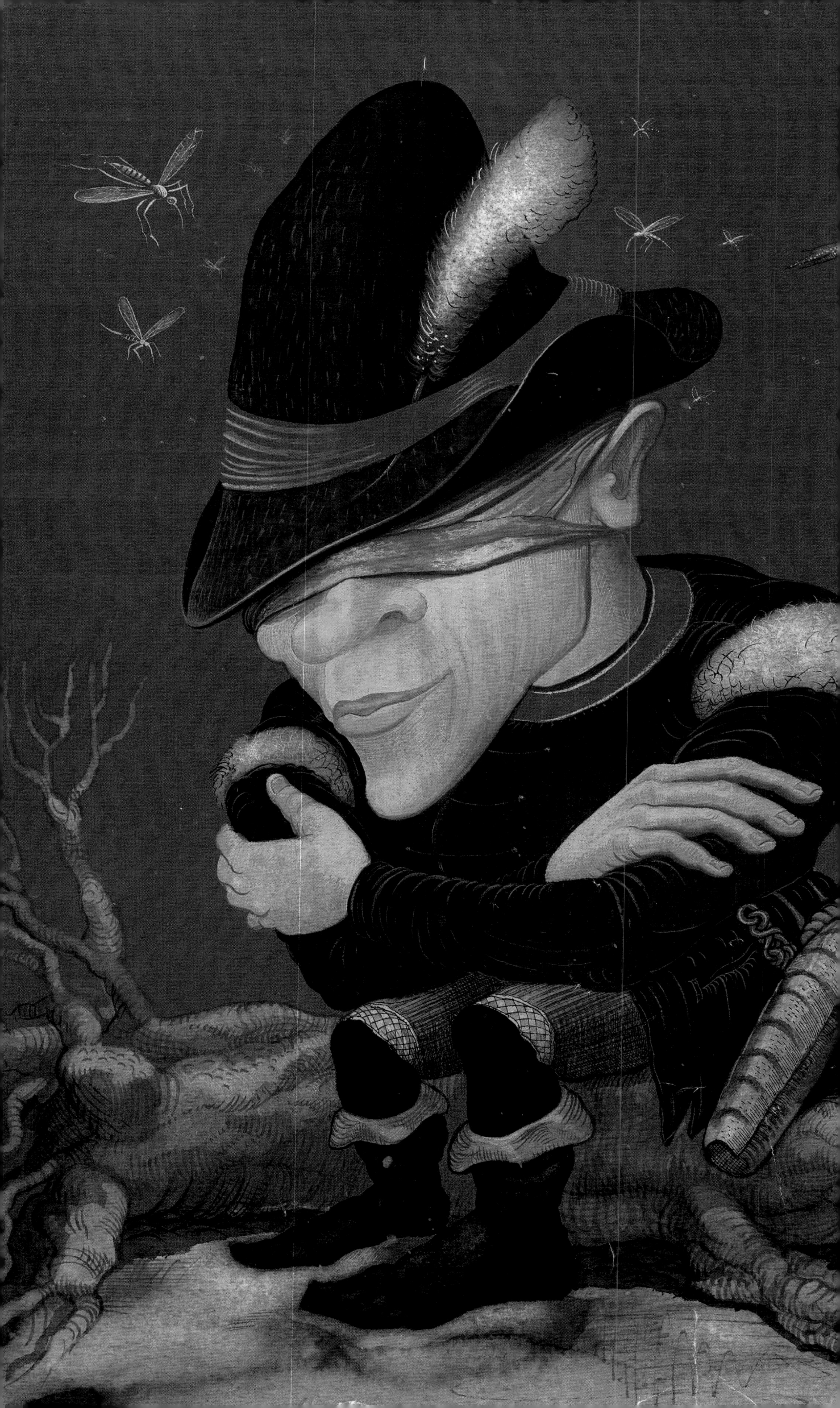

On they went, and they met a man sitting by the road with his eyes blindfolded.

"Are your eyes too weak to stand the daylight?" asked the prince.

"No," said the man, "but I mustn't take off this blindfold, because my glance is so powerful, anything I look at breaks into pieces. If that's any use to you, I'll be happy to serve you."

"I think I can use your services," said the prince, "so come along with me."

They went on again, and they came
to a man lying in the hot sunlight
and shaking all over with cold.

"How can you be cold," asked the prince,
"when the sun's so hot today?"

"Oh," said the man, "I'm not the same as other people.
The hotter it is, the colder I feel, so that I can't stop
shivering. And the colder it is, the hotter I feel. I can't
bear frost because it makes me so hot, and I can't bear
fire because it makes me so cold."

"Well," said the prince, "you're a strange fellow, but if
you'd like to be my servant, then come along with me."

So they went on, and saw a man craning his long, long
neck, looking over all the mountaintops.

"What are you looking at?" asked the prince.

"I have such sharp eyes," said the man, "that I can
see over the forests and the mountains. I can see right
through the world."

"Then I believe I could do with you," said the prince,
"so if you'd like to be my servant, just come along
with me."

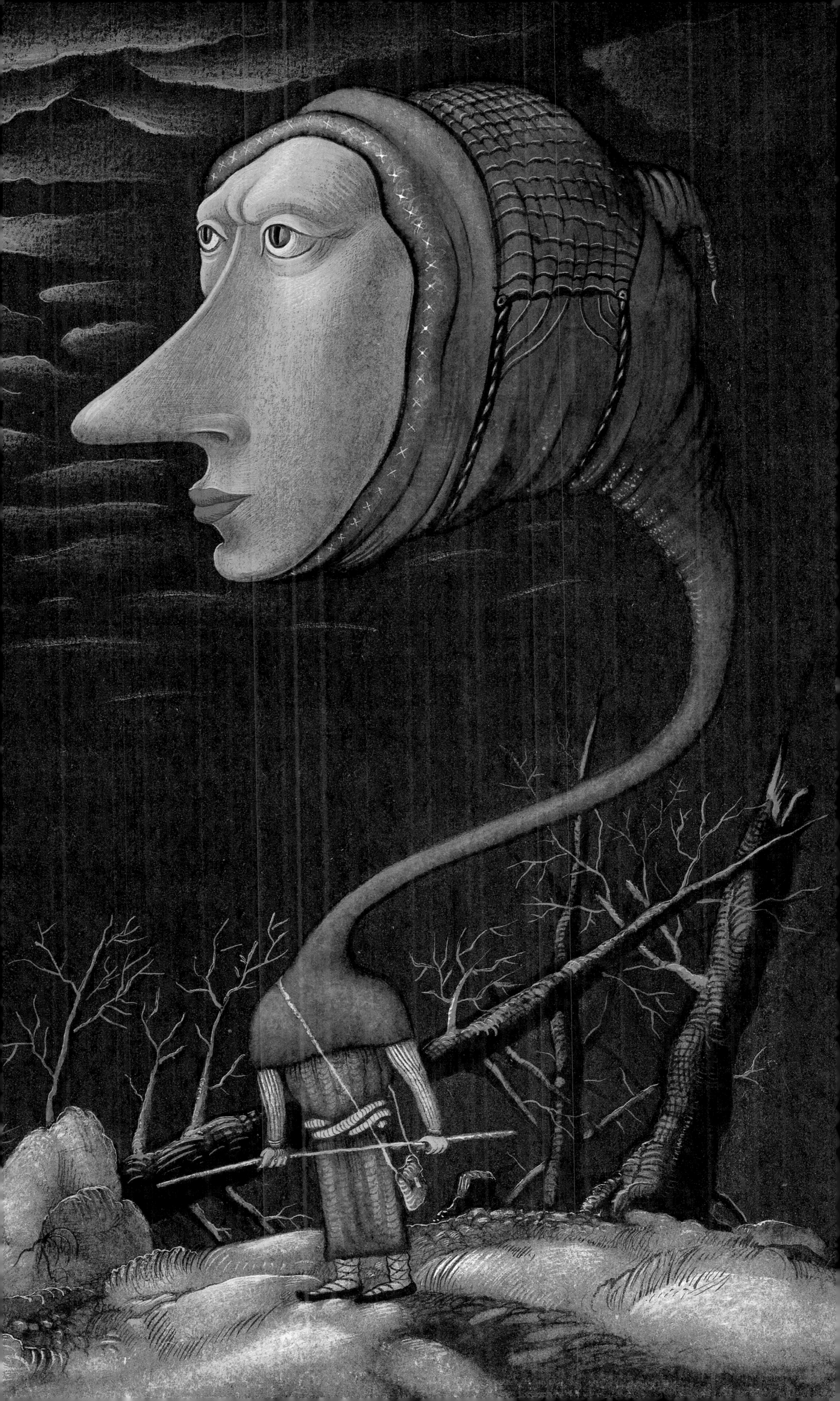

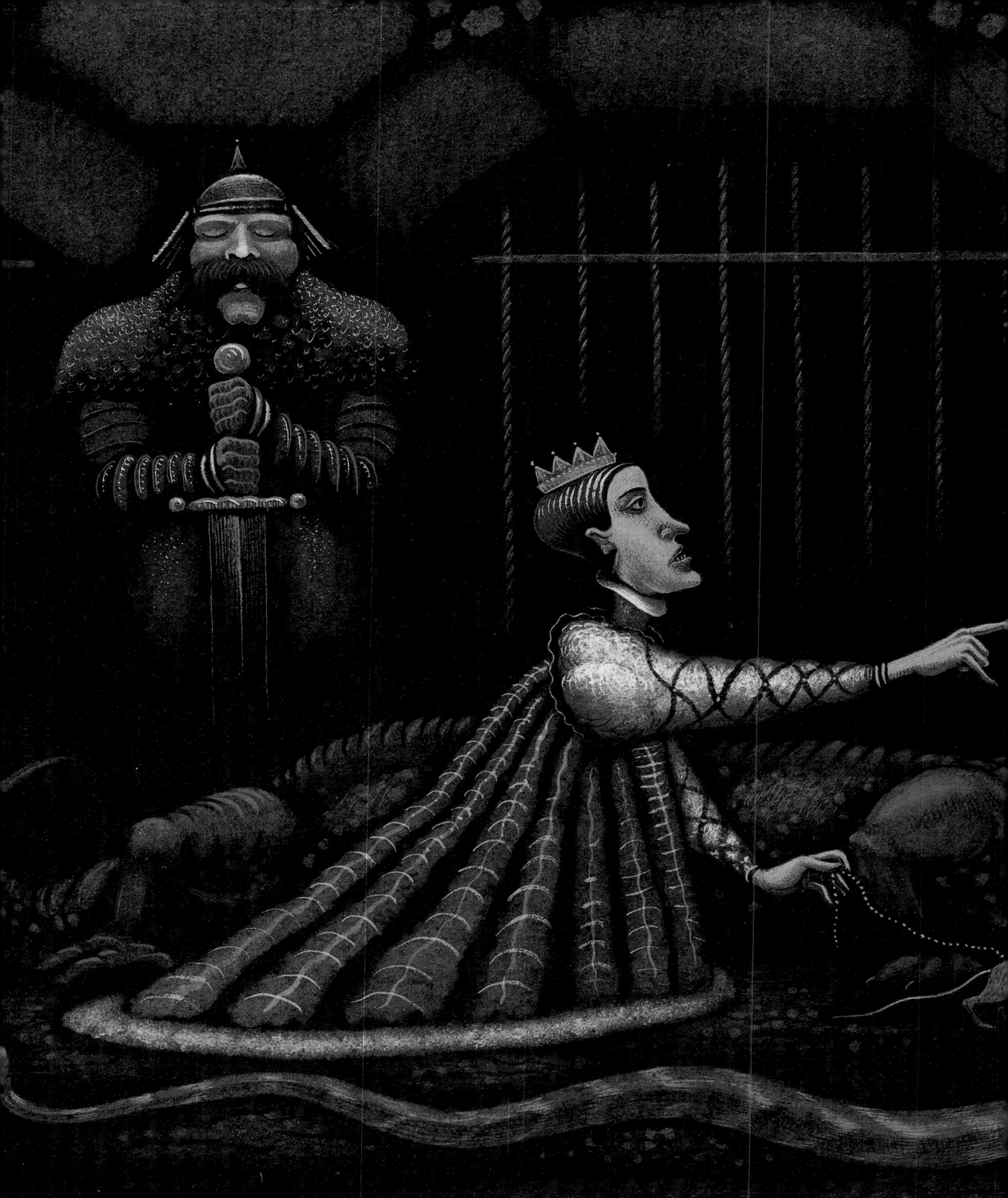

So the prince and his six servants came to the city where the old queen lived. The prince did not say who he was, but he told the queen, "Give me your lovely daughter, and I'll perform any task you set me."

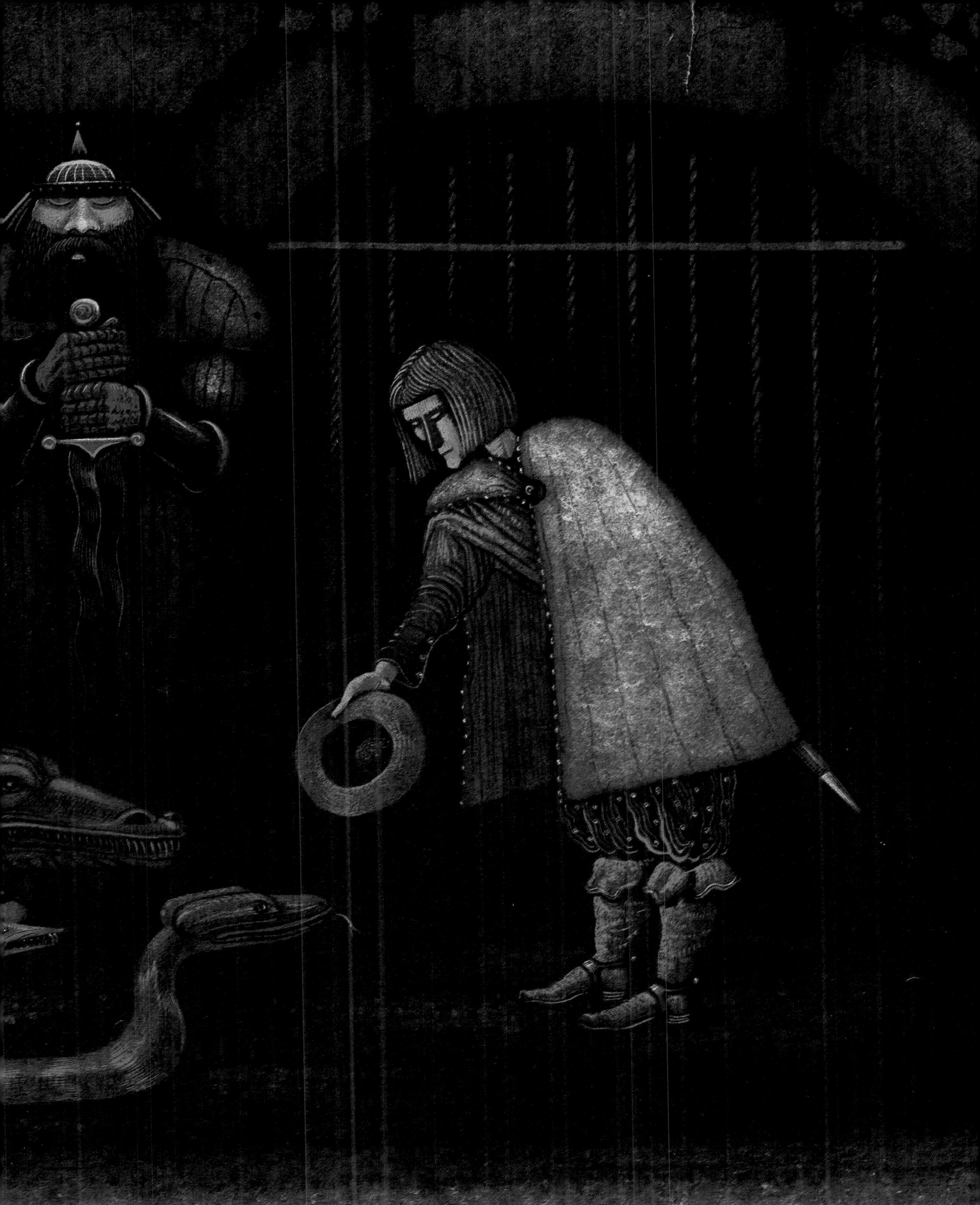

Glad to see yet another handsome young man fall into her clutches, the enchantress said, "I will set you three tasks, and if you perform them all, you may marry my daughter."

"What's the first task?" he asked.

"You must bring me a ring I once dropped in the Red Sea," said the queen.

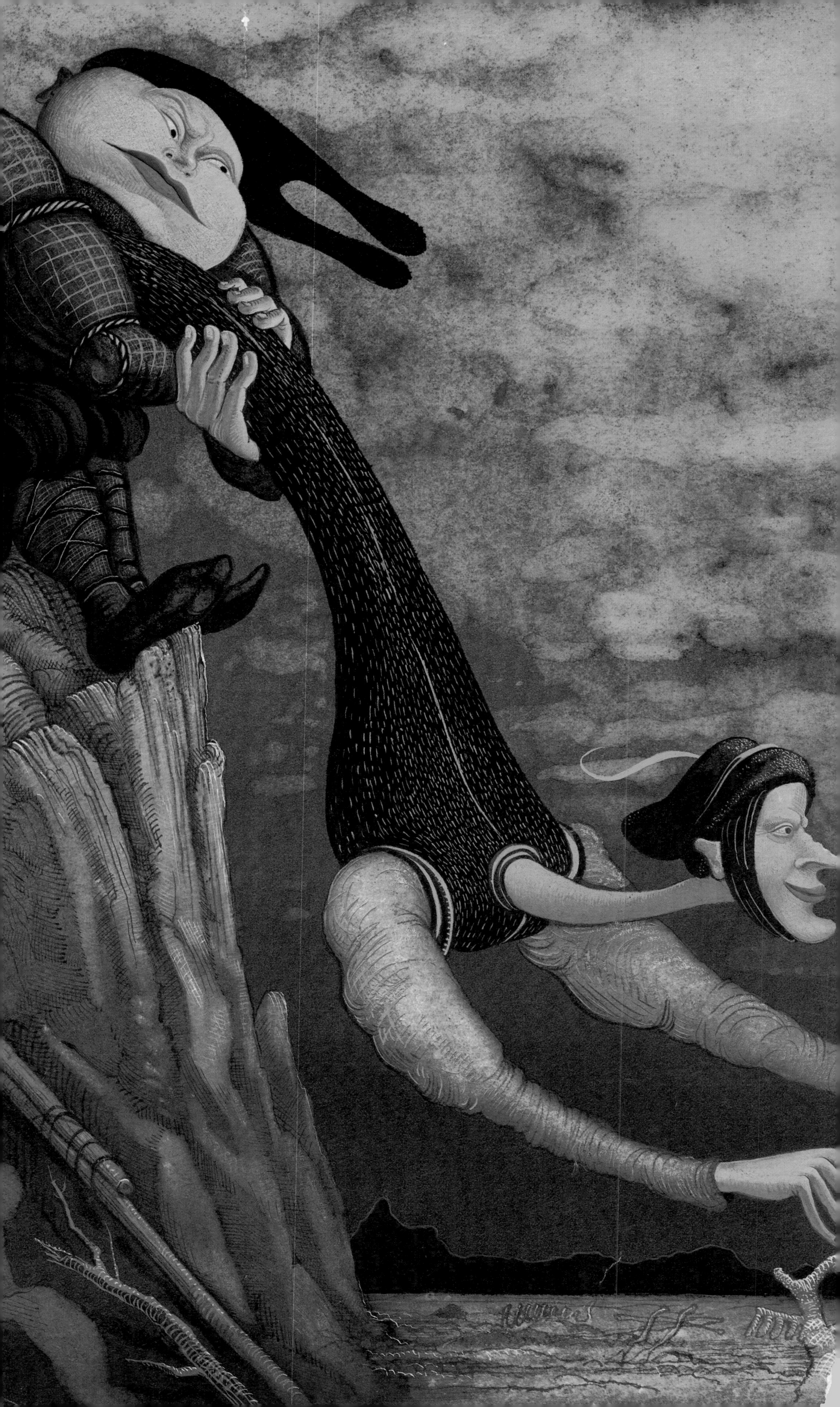

The prince went back to his servants, and told them, "The first task is a hard one. I have to fetch the queen a ring she dropped in the Red Sea. What do you suggest?"

The man with sharp eyes said, "Let me see where it is." He looked down into the Red Sea and said, "It's hanging on a pointed rock."

The tall man carried them there and said, "I'd fish it out if only I could see it."

"If that's all, just wait!" said the fat man, and he lay down and let the water flow into his mouth. He drank up the whole Red Sea until it was as dry as a meadow. Then the tall man bent a little way and picked up the ring.

The prince was glad to have the ring, and he took it to the old queen, who was amazed.

"Do you see the three hundred fat oxen grazing in the pastures outside my castle?" asked the queen. "You must eat them up, skin, bone, hair, horns and all. And there are three hundred barrels of wine down in my cellar. You must drink them with the meal. If you leave as much as a single hair from one of the oxen or a single drop of wine, you die!"

"May I invite any guests?" asked the prince. "No meal tastes any good without company."

The old woman gave a nasty laugh and said, "You may invite one guest to keep you company, but only one."

So the prince went to his servants and told the fat man, "You will be my guest today, and eat as much as you want for once."

Then the fat man puffed himself out, ate the three hundred oxen, leaving not a hair behind, and asked what else there was for dinner. As for the wine, he didn't drink it from a glass, but straight from the barrels, and licked up the very last drop.

When he had finished, the prince went to the old woman and told her that the second task had been performed. She was astonished, and said, "No one ever got as far as this before, but you still have one task left." This time, she thought, he would never escape, and his head would be cut off.

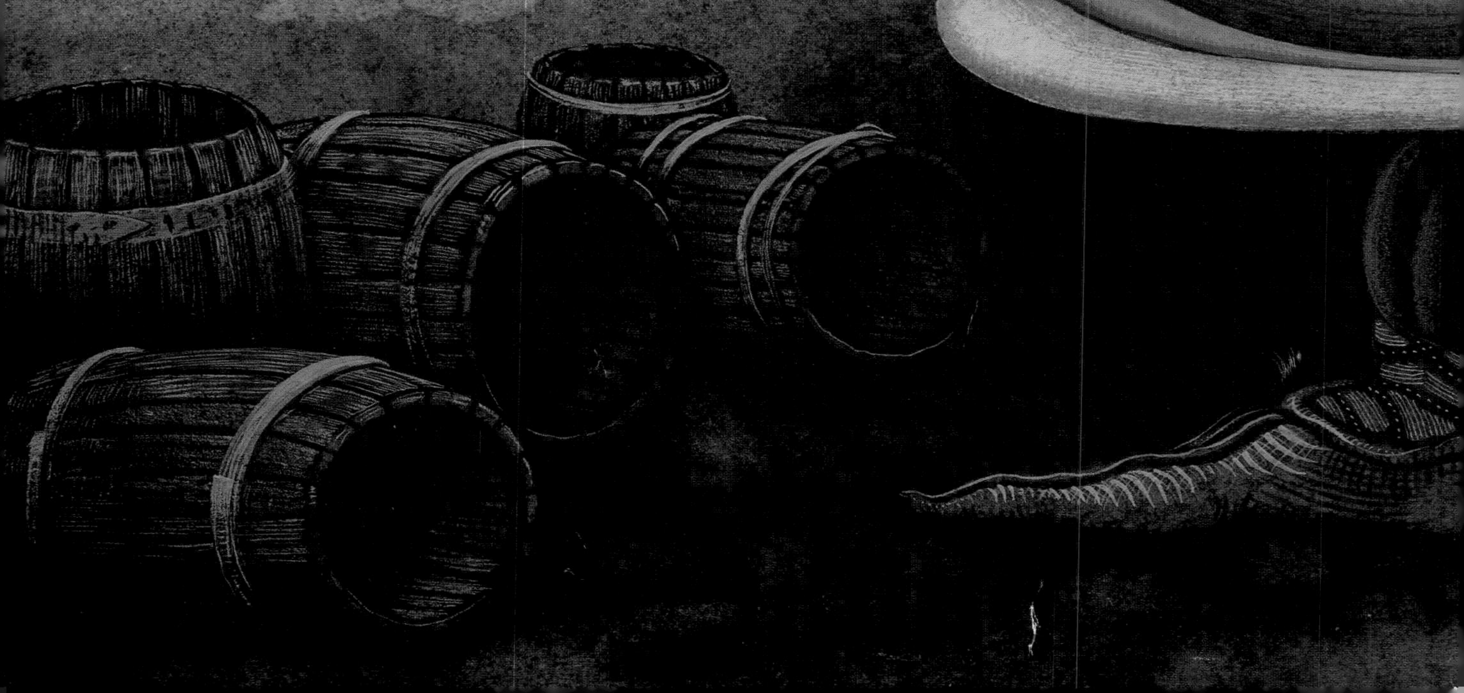

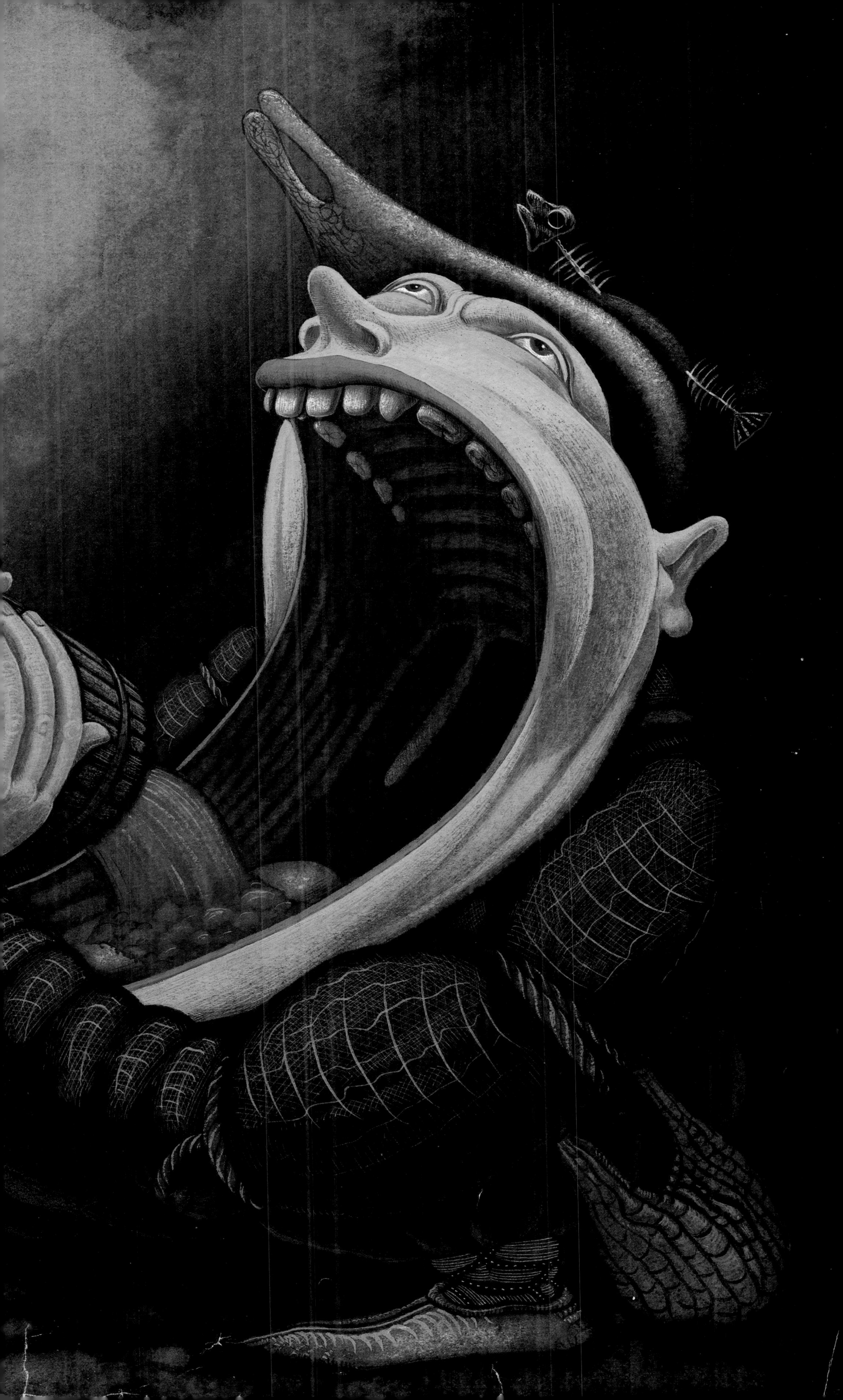

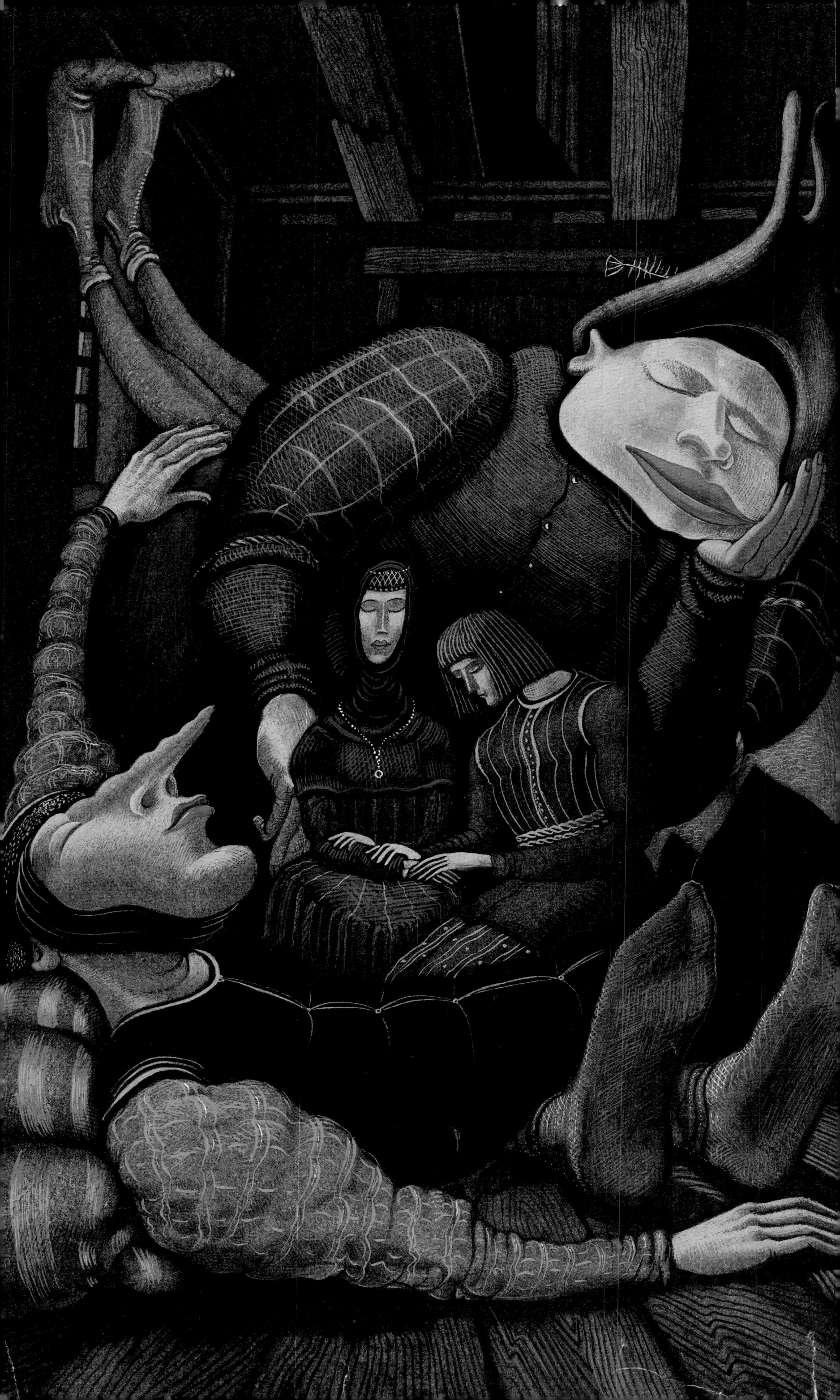

I will bring my daughter to your room this evening," she said. "You may hold her in your arms, but make sure you don't fall asleep. I'll come back on the stroke of midnight, and if she isn't still in your arms, you've lost."

The prince thought this was an easy task, and he would be sure to keep his eyes open, but he called his servants, told them about the task, and said, "Who knows what cunning trick may be behind it? Better safe than sorry! So keep watch, and make sure the girl doesn't leave my room."

When night fell, the old woman brought her daughter and put her in the prince's arms. The tall man coiled himself around them in a circle, and the fat man stationed himself at the door so that no living soul could pass. There the two of them sat, and the girl never spoke a word, but the moonlight shone through the window and fell on her face, showing the prince her wonderful beauty. He did nothing but gaze at her in love and joy, and not a trace of weariness came into his eyes. So they sat there until eleven o'clock, when the old woman cast a spell to make everyone fall asleep, and at that moment the girl disappeared.

They all slept soundly until a quarter to twelve, when the magic spell wore off and they woke up again.

"Alas!" cried the prince. "I am a dead man!"

His faithful servants began to weep, except for the man with the keen ears, who said, "Hush. I want to listen." He listened for a moment, and then he said, "The princess is sitting inside a rock, three hundred hours' journey from here, lamenting her fate. You're the only one who can help us, Lofty. Stretch out as tall as you can, and a few steps will take you there."

"True," said the tall man, "but our blindfolded friend must come with me to break the rock with his powerful eyes."

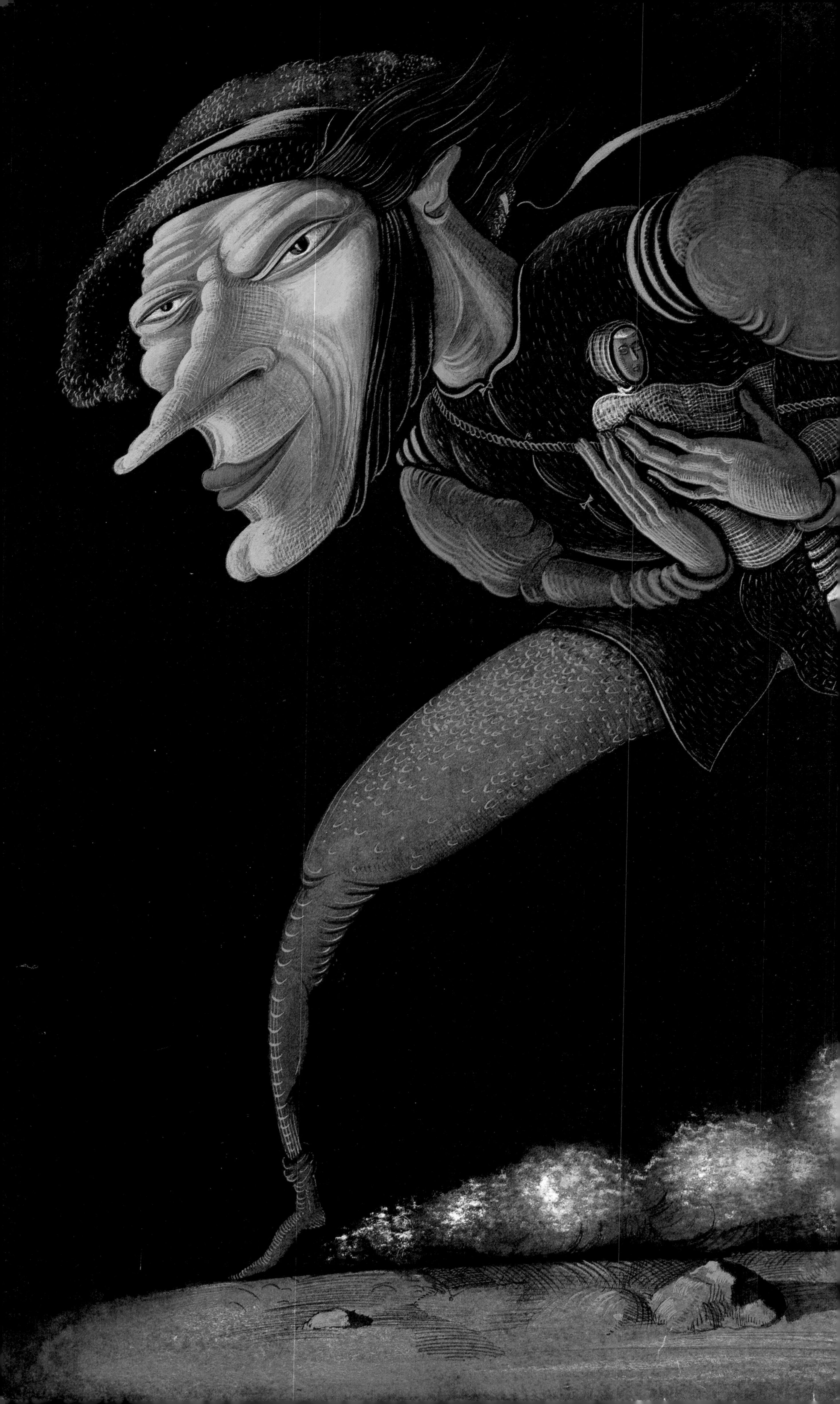

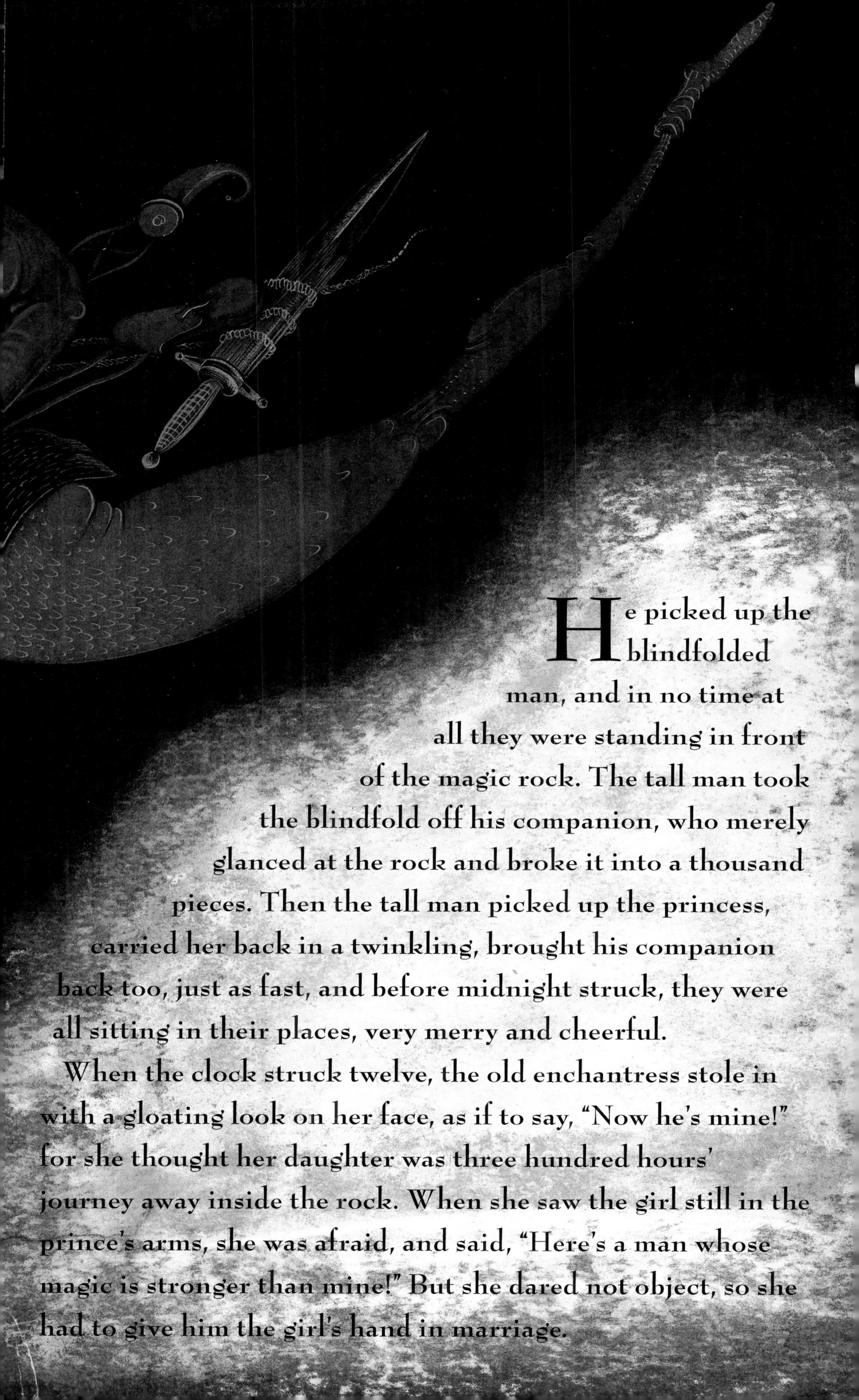

He picked up the blindfolded man, and in no time at all they were standing in front of the magic rock. The tall man took the blindfold off his companion, who merely glanced at the rock and broke it into a thousand pieces. Then the tall man picked up the princess, carried her back in a twinkling, brought his companion back too, just as fast, and before midnight struck, they were all sitting in their places, very merry and cheerful.

When the clock struck twelve, the old enchantress stole in with a gloating look on her face, as if to say, "Now he's mine!" for she thought her daughter was three hundred hours' journey away inside the rock. When she saw the girl still in the prince's arms, she was afraid, and said, "Here's a man whose magic is stronger than mine!" But she dared not object, so she had to give him the girl's hand in marriage.

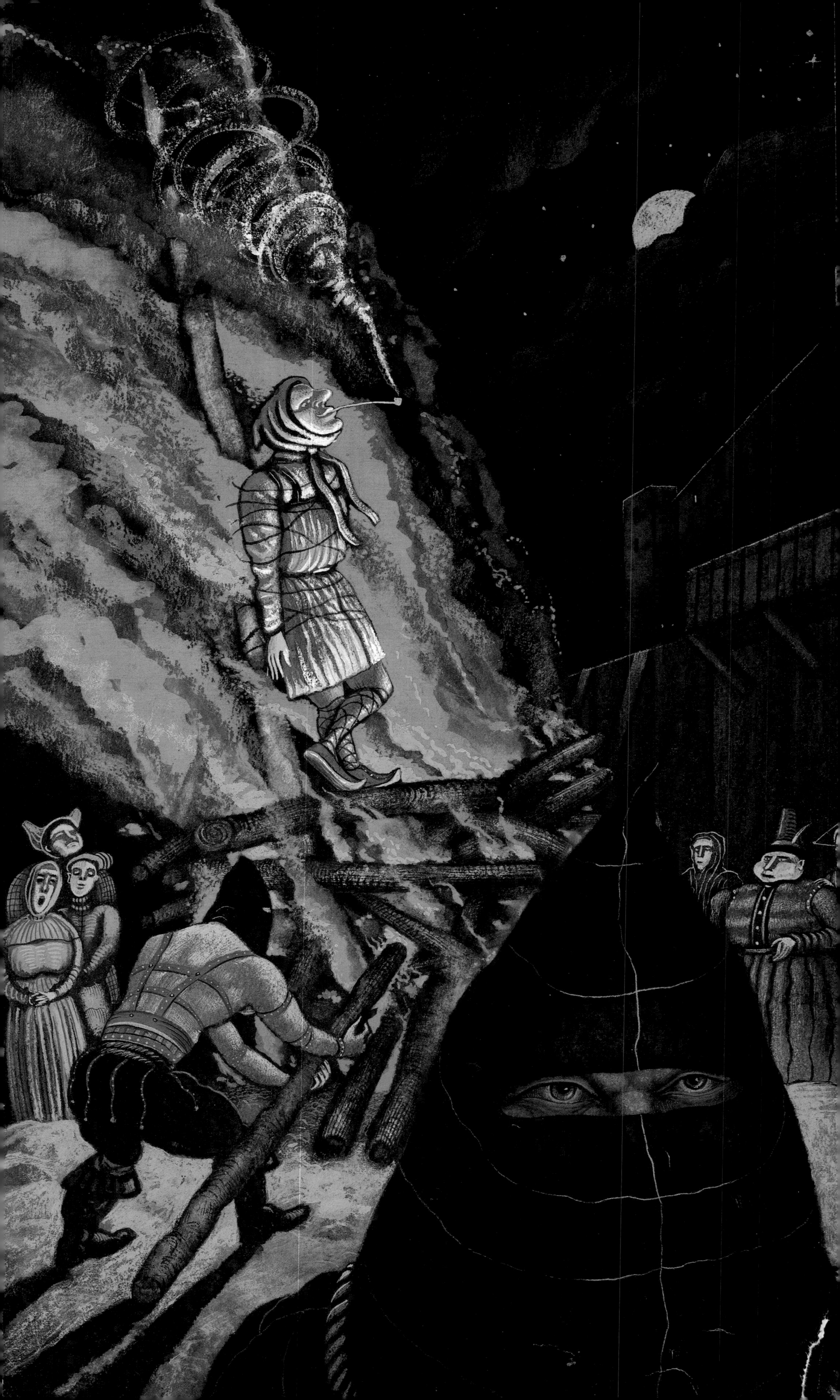

However, she whispered in the princess's ear, "Shame on you, taking a common man in marriage instead of a husband to your own liking!"

Then the girl's proud heart was filled with anger, and she thought of revenge. Next morning, she had three hundred bundles of firewood built into a bonfire, and she told the prince that although he had performed the three tasks, she wouldn't be his wife unless he could find someone prepared to sit in the middle of the bonfire and bear the heat of it. She thought none of his servants would burn to death for him, so he would go into the flames himself for love of her, and then she would be free.

But the servants said, "We've all done something except for the shivering man. It's his turn now." So they put him in the middle of the firewood and lit it. Then the bonfire began to burn. It burned for three days, until all the wood was gone, and when the flames died down, there stood the shivering man in the middle of the ashes, trembling like an aspen leaf, and saying, "I've never known such bitter cold in all my life. If it had gone on any longer, I'd have frozen to death."

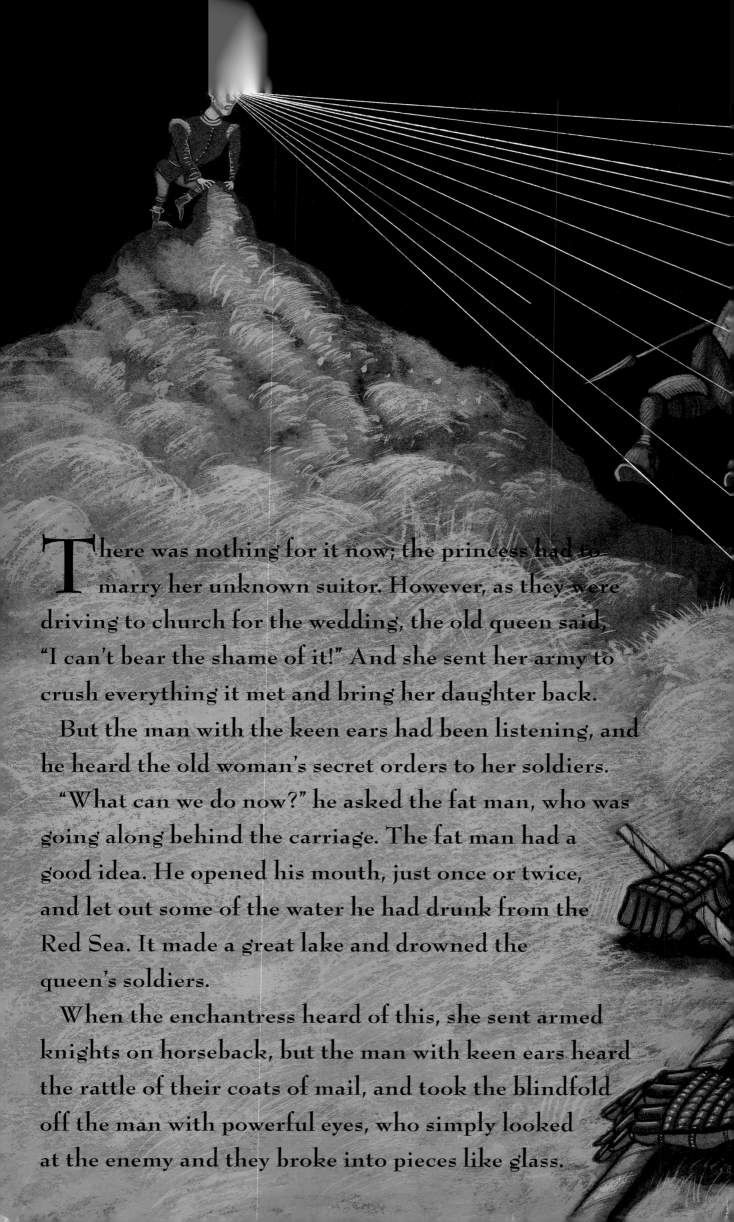

There was nothing for it now; the princess had to
marry her unknown suitor. However, as they were
driving to church for the wedding, the old queen said,
"I can't bear the shame of it!" And she sent her army to
crush everything it met and bring her daughter back.

But the man with the keen ears had been listening, and
he heard the old woman's secret orders to her soldiers.

"What can we do now?" he asked the fat man, who was
going along behind the carriage. The fat man had a
good idea. He opened his mouth, just once or twice,
and let out some of the water he had drunk from the
Red Sea. It made a great lake and drowned the
queen's soldiers.

When the enchantress heard of this, she sent armed
knights on horseback, but the man with keen ears heard
the rattle of their coats of mail, and took the blindfold
off the man with powerful eyes, who simply looked
at the enemy and they broke into pieces like glass.

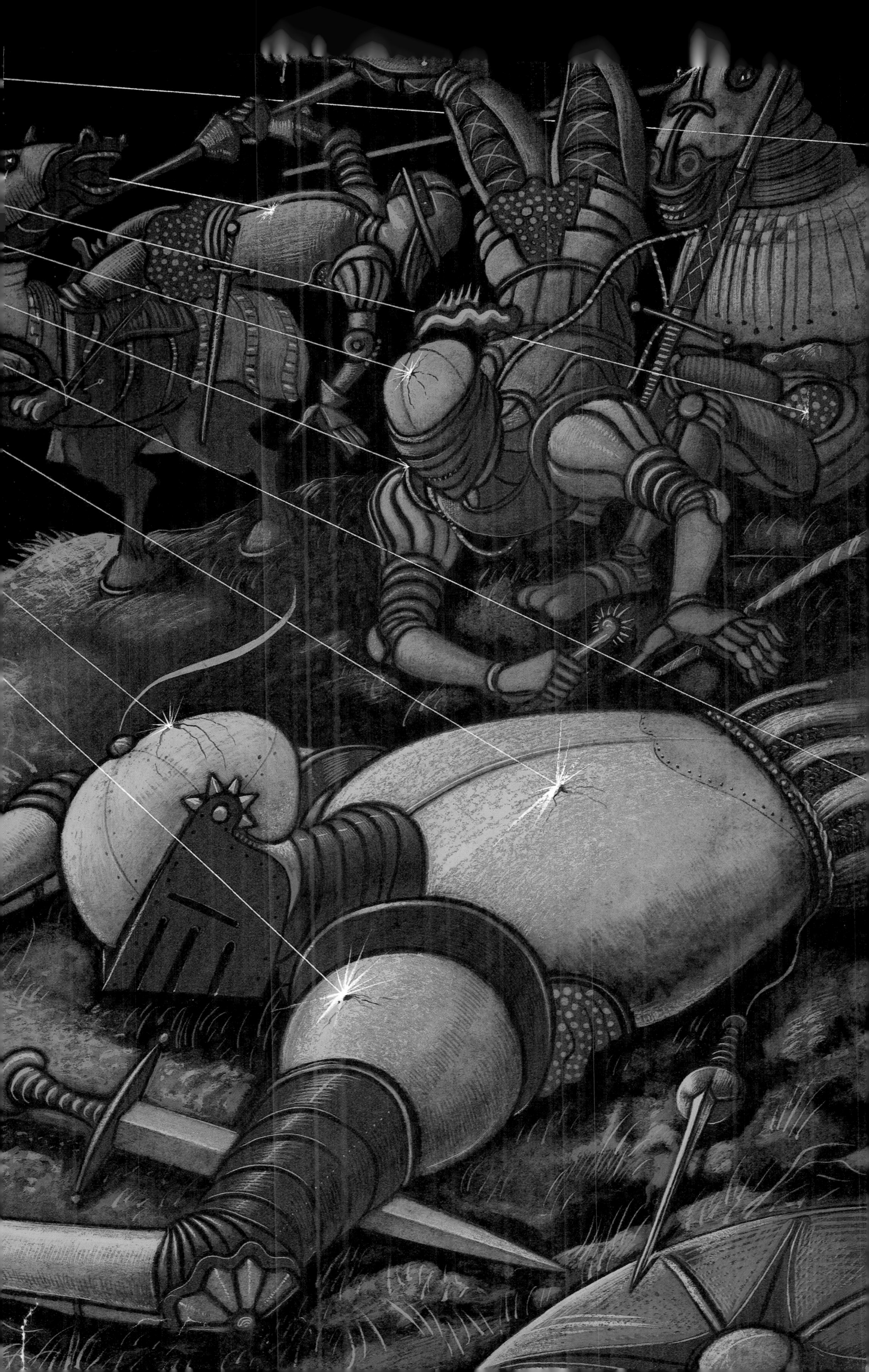

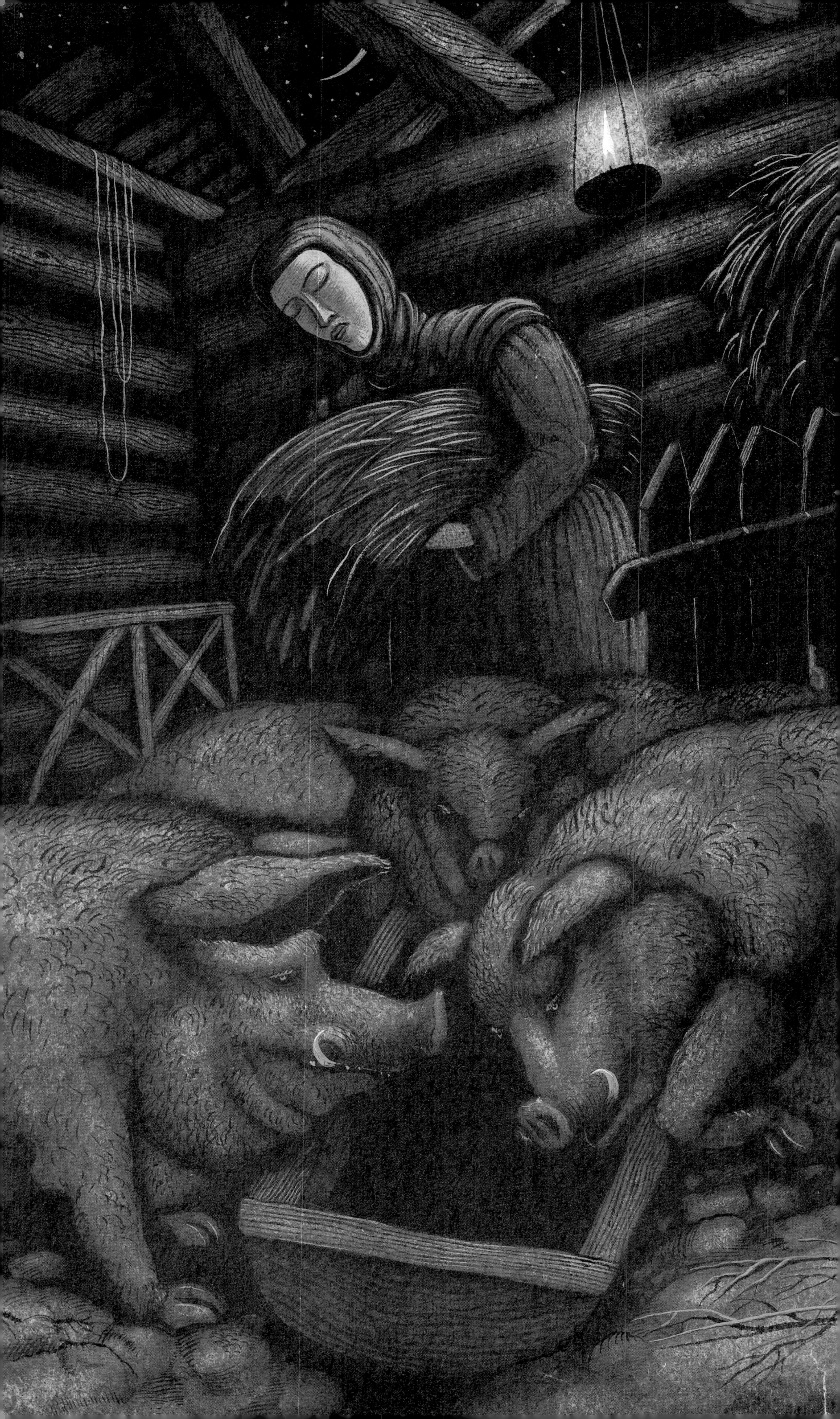

Now the wedding party drove on undisturbed, and when the young couple had been married in church, the six servants said good-bye, telling their master, "Your wishes have all been granted and you don't need us anymore, so we'll go on our way and seek our fortunes."

Half an hour's journey from the king's castle there was a village, where the newly married couple saw a swineherd with his pigs. As they came closer, the prince said to his wife, "Do you know who I really am? I'm a swineherd, and the man with the pigs over there is my father. The two of us must go and help him with his work."

Then he took her into an inn, and secretly told the inn-keepers to take her royal clothes away during the night. When she woke up in the morning, she had nothing to wear, so the landlady gave her an old dress and a pair of wool stockings, acting as if they were a magnificent present. "But for your husband, I wouldn't have given you anything at all," she said.

So the princess believed he really was a swineherd, and went to look after the pigs, thinking, "I deserve it for being so proud and haughty."

This went on for eight days, until her feet hurt so much that she could bear it no longer.

Just then some men came along and asked if she knew who her husband was.

"Yes," she said, "He is a swineherd, and he's just gone out to earn a little extra money selling ribbons and laces."

"Come with us," they said, "and we'll take you to him."

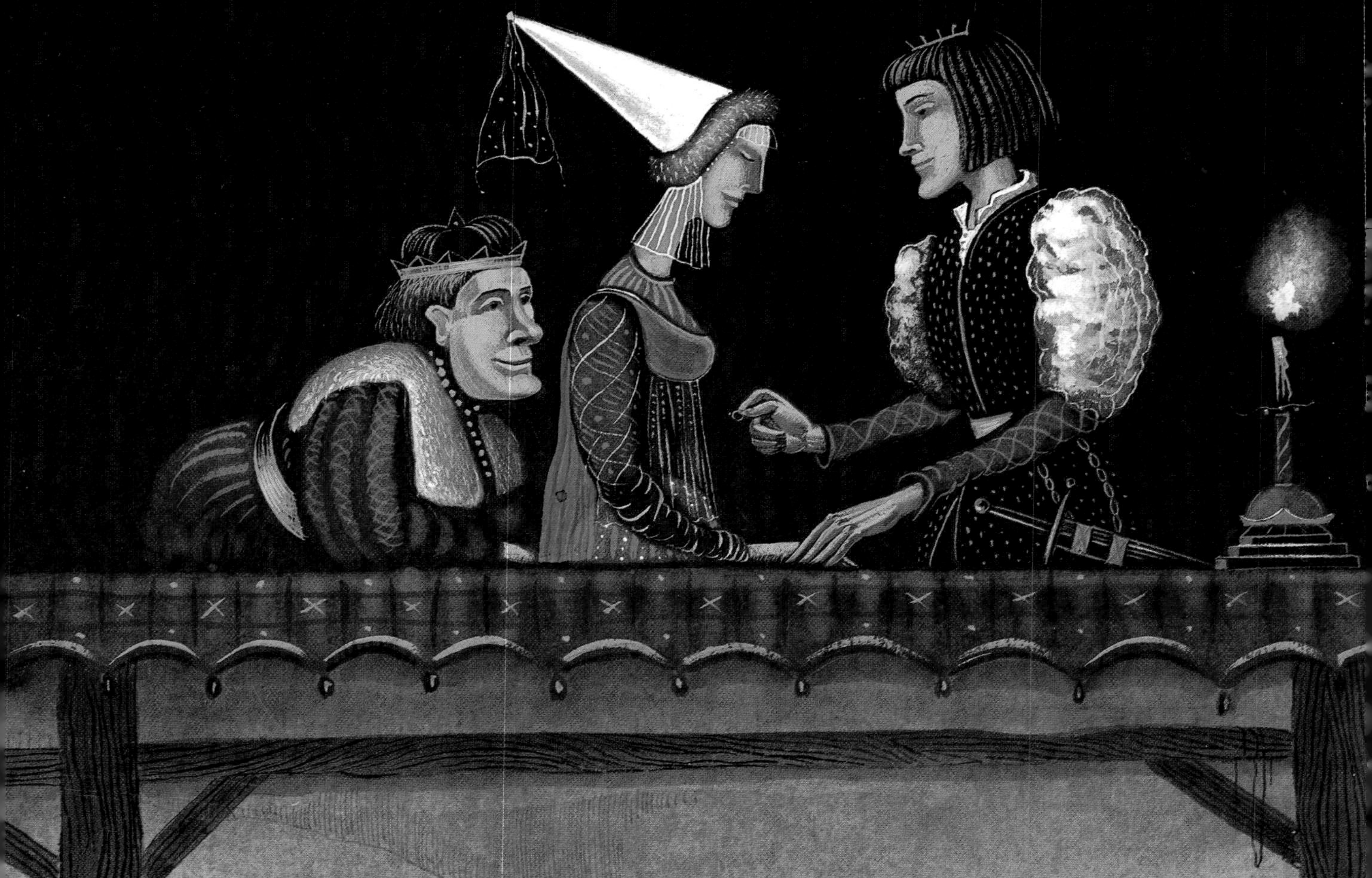

They took her to the castle, and as she came into the great hall, she saw her husband dressed in magnificent robes. She did not recognize him until he put his arms around her, kissed her, and said, "I suffered so much for you, and now you have suffered for me, too."

So then they held a grand wedding feast, and I wish I had been there myself!

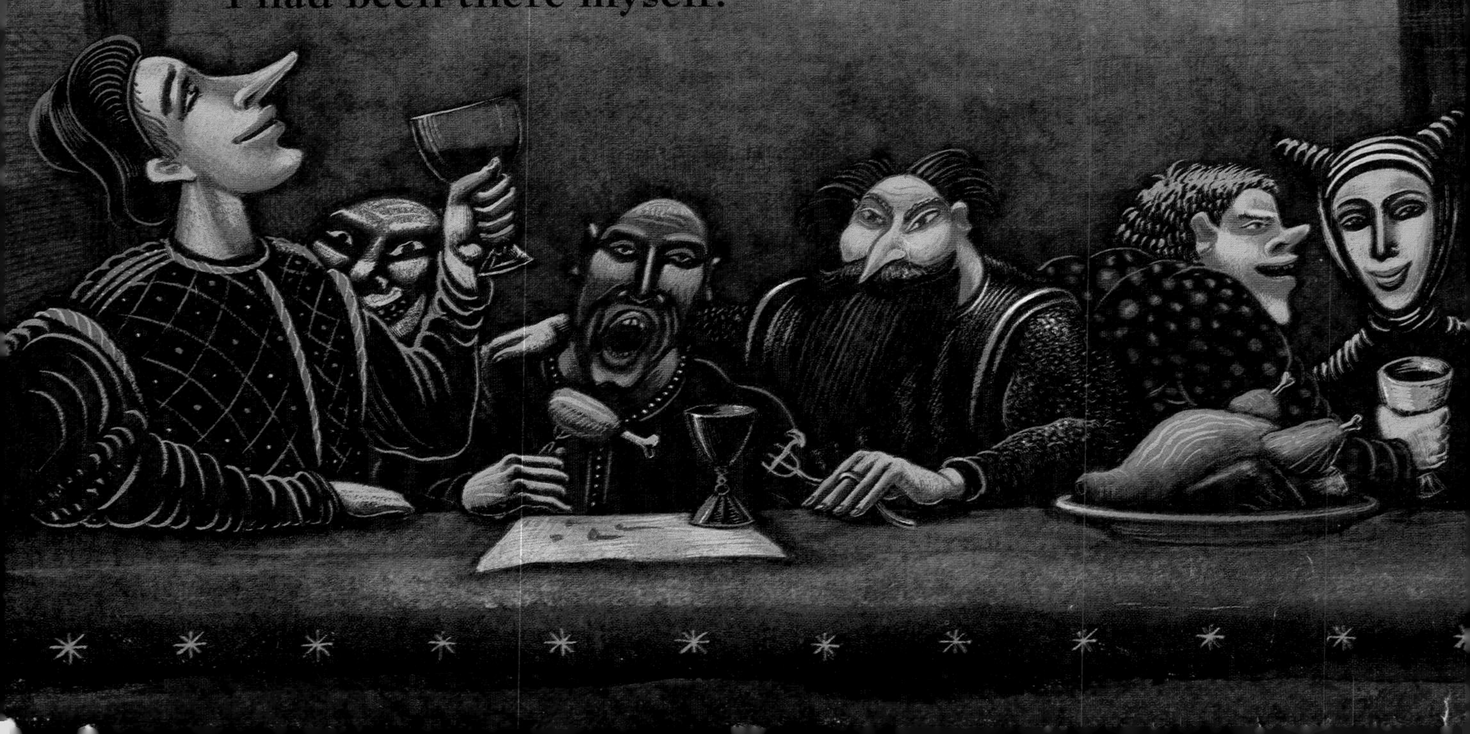